My Ocean is Blue

To Michelle — D.L.

To Meribeth and Carol Anne, for taking Jessi, Jen
and me to the beach every summer — A.B.

Kids Can Press gratefully acknowledges the financial support of the
Government of Ontario, through Ontario Creates; the Ontario Arts Council;
the Canada Council for the Arts; and the Government of Canada for our
publishing activity.

Published in Canada and the U.S. by Kids Can Press Ltd.
25 Dockside Drive, Toronto, ON M5A 0B5

Kids Can Press is a Corus Entertainment Inc. company

www.kidscanpress.com

The artwork in this book was rendered in cut-paper collage, watercolor,
acrylic and pencil crayon, with some digital assembly.
The text is set in Cambria.

Edited by Jennifer Stokes
Designed by Julia Naimska

Printed and bound in Malaysia in 10/2019 by Tien Wah Press (Pte.) Ltd.

MIX
Paper from
responsible sources
FSC® C012700
FSC
www.fsc.org

CM 20 0 9 8 7 6 5 4 3 2 1

Library and Archives Canada Cataloguing in Publication

Title: My ocean is blue / written by Darren Lebeuf ; illustrated by Ashley Barron
Names: Lebeuf, Darren, author. | Barron, Ashley, illustrator.
Identifiers: Canadiana 20190097620 | ISBN 9781525301438 (hardcover)
Classification: LCC PS8623.E254 M9 2020 | DDC jC813/.6 — dc23

My Ocean is Blue

Written by Darren Lebeuf

Illustrated by Ashley Barron

Kids Can Press

This is my ocean.

And *this* is my ocean.

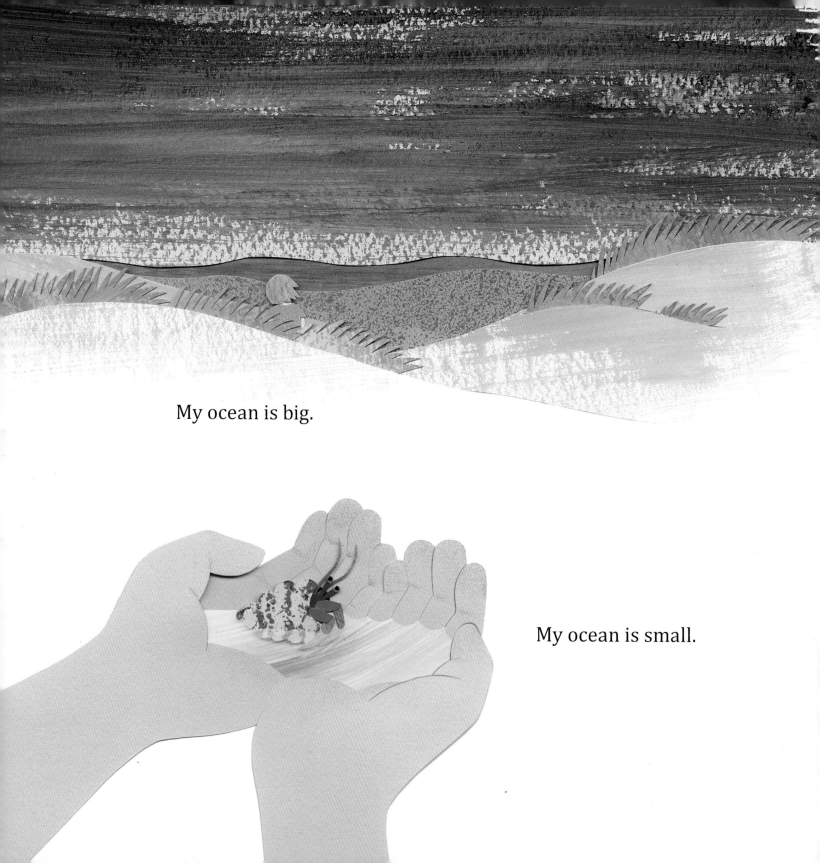

My ocean is big.

My ocean is small.

My ocean is shallow.

My ocean is deep.

My ocean is slimy

and sandy

and sparkly and dull.

My ocean is dotted
and spiraled

and wavy and straight.

Sometimes my ocean is dry.

Sometimes it's wet.

Sometimes it's rotten,

and sometimes it's fresh.

My ocean splashes and crashes
and echoes and squawks.

My ocean laughs and hums.

But, at times, it's silent.

My ocean appears ...

and disappears.

It bobs and skips and jumps and sinks.

My ocean is blue.
Deep blue, quiet blue,

loud blue,

endless blue.

My ocean is also
vibrant pink,

rusted orange,

faded white,

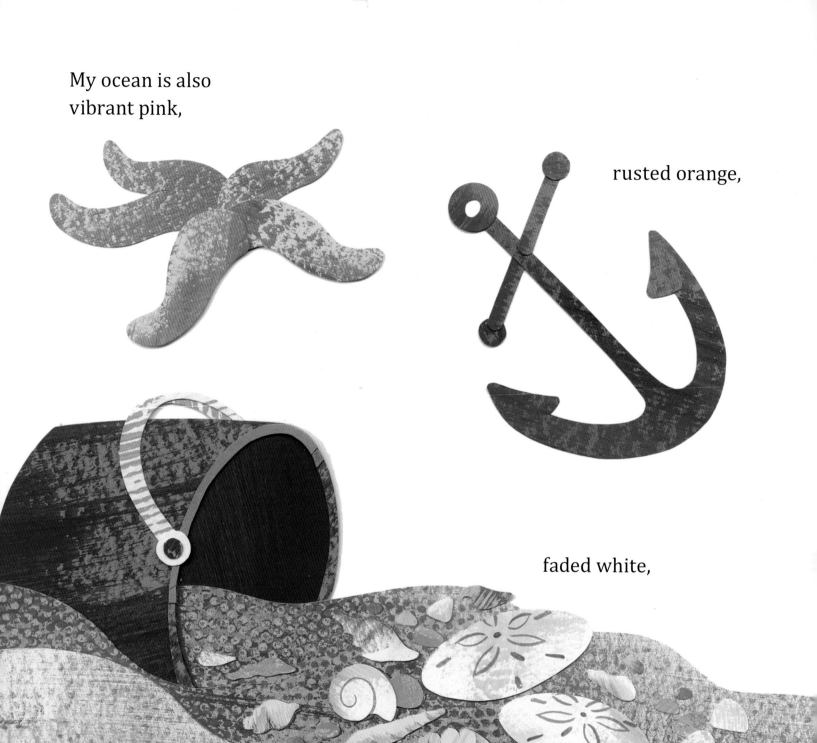

balanced gray,

runaway red

and polished green.

But mostly it's blue.

My ocean is always different ...

I wonder what my ocean
will be tomorrow.